CARS, TRUCKS AND MUSCLE CARS

COLORING BOOK FOR BOYS

BY

LUCKY COLORS

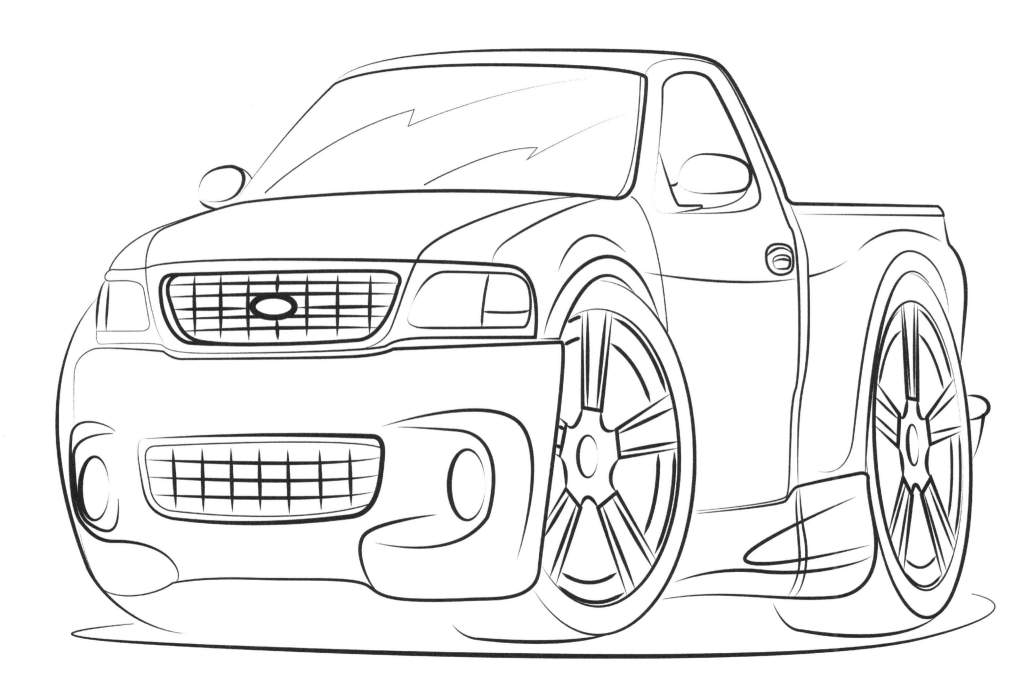

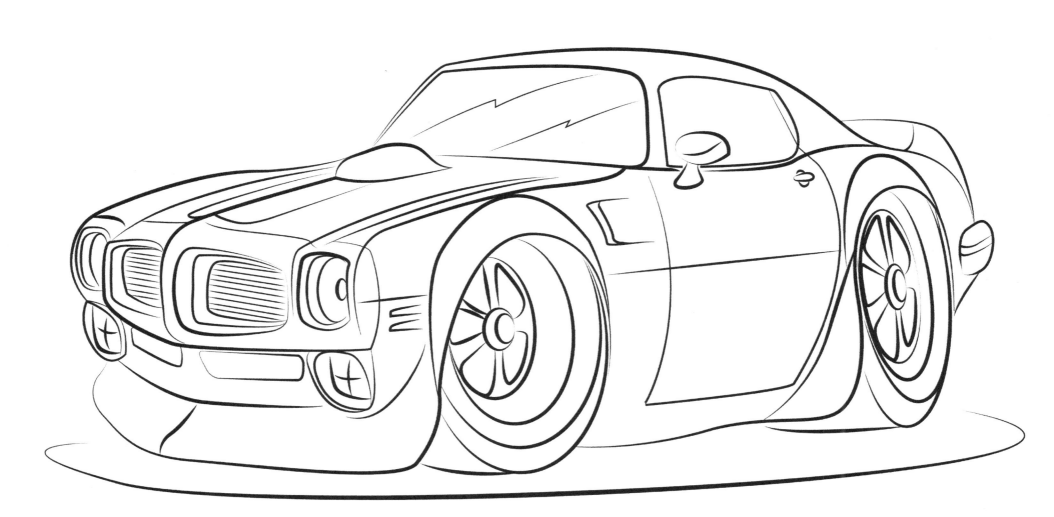

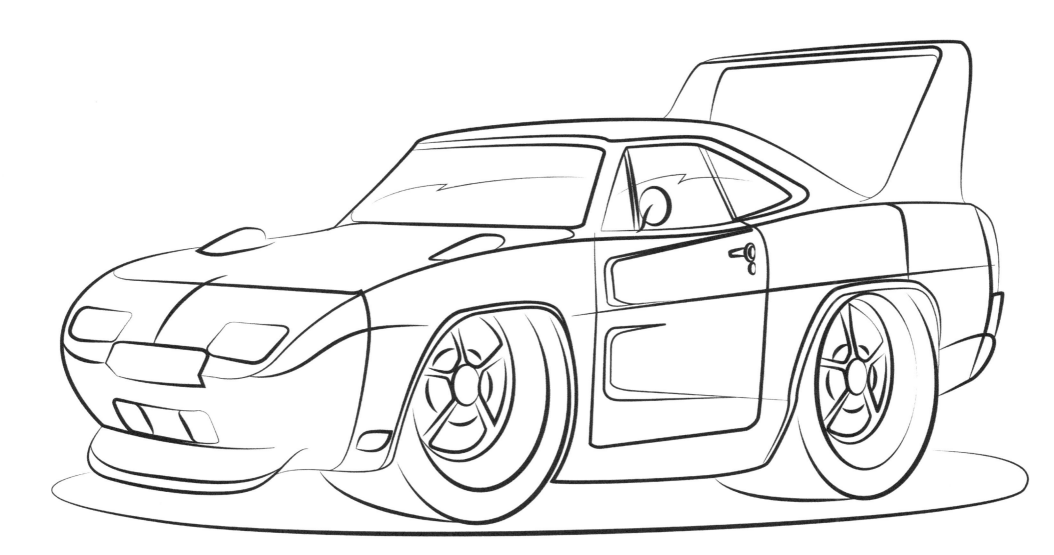

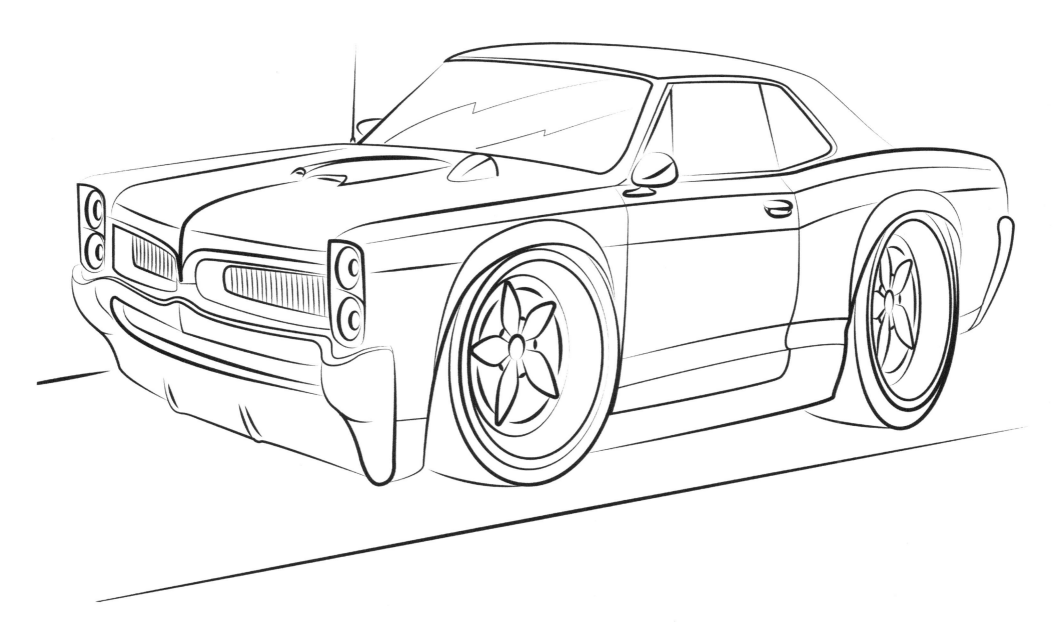

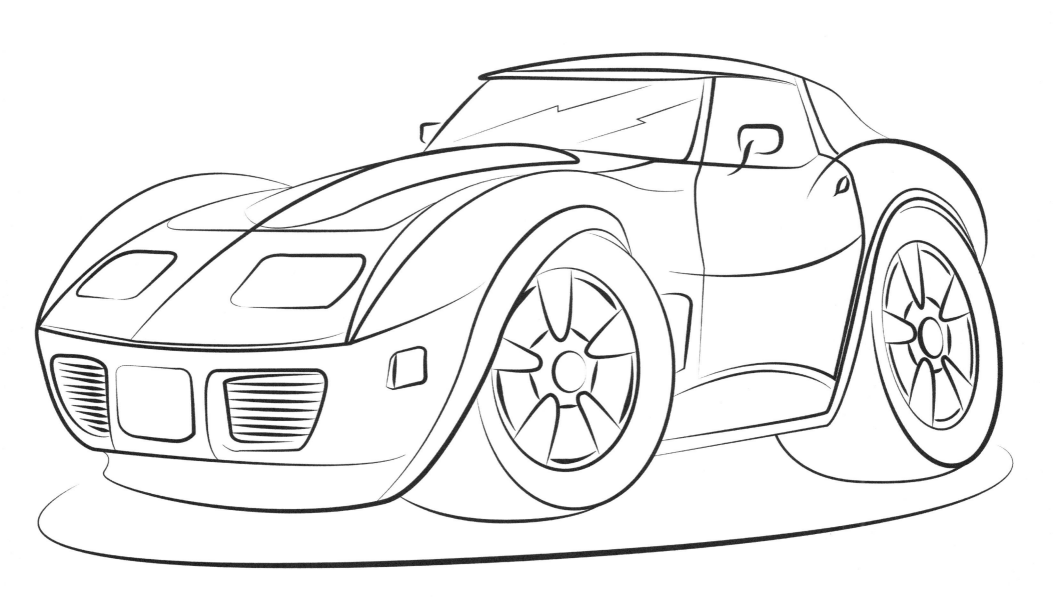

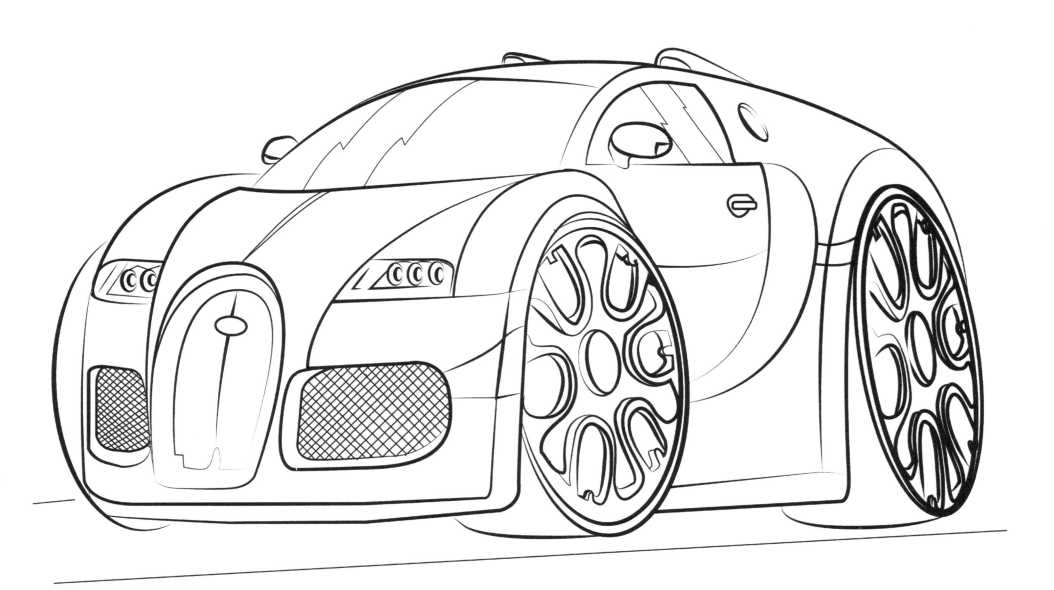

Our new book is already on sale! A great gift for the little ones!

ISBN: 979-8577539610

Thank you for choosing our book!
We hope the book will be very useful and joyful for your child!
We will be happy to receive your feedback)

Made in the USA
Middletown, DE
01 September 2023

37789465R00071